'Twas the Week Before Christmas

by

Teresa Kelly
&

Wendy Winger

'Twas the Week Before Christmas

Highview Press Incorporated
2122 Highview Drive
Burlington, Ontario L7R 3X4

ISBN 0 - 9680443 -0 -1   Printed in Canada

Acknowledgments

*We dedicate this book to our husbands, Brendan and Carl,
for their unstinting support and their endless patience.*

The idea for this book was born in a flash of inspiration and was nurtured to fruition by our love of Christmas, family and tradition. The two-year task of compiling and presenting this potpourri of holiday gems was lightened and enriched by the loving assistance of family and friends who shared their treasured recipes, craft ideas and decorating skills. It is therefore with pleasure and gratitude that we acknowledge these contributors: Brenda Gatley, for her cheesy crab appetizers (p. 12), Russ Bays, for his celebrated cheddar cheese dip (p. 12), and Justine Morris for her Acadian Tourtière (p. 20) — a treasured legacy from her Acadian ancestors. Our thanks also to Eleanor Tremblay for sharing her very own recipe for a banana bread (p. 31) that we've enjoyed for over a quarter of a century! We are indebted also to Hilda and Gary Cusson for their two gastronomic delights — lemon squares (p. 25) and bacon and cheese muffins (p. 32).

The beautiful mailbox which adorns our house and is featured on page 49 was a generous gift from Bob Gatley who, in the true spirit of Christmas, designed and built it for us as a surprise Christmas gift! The very popular eye-catching quilted Christmas cards presented on page 67 and meticulously described on pages 68 and 69 are the creation of Linda Franz who has graciously shared with us her talent and techniques. We are pleased to thank Andrea Mori-Mickus for granting us permission to publish our photograph of her beautifully decorated house (p. 35) which captured the spirit of the holiday season and our attention.

A special debt of gratitude is acknowledged to our families. We thank the members of the Kelly family, Brendan, Aaron, and Shannon, for testing recipes, creating crafts, and providing moral support during two years of making, baking and photographing. We also wish to thank Brendan for his computer layout and design contributions. To the Winger family, Carl, Kevin and Adrian, we say "thank you" for enduring a house full of Christmas decorations twelve months a year!

Table Of Contents

Recipes

Table Of Contents

Decorations

Table Of Contents
Crafts, Gift Ideas & Kids' Crafts

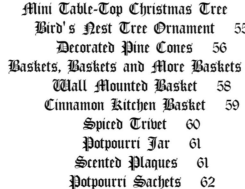

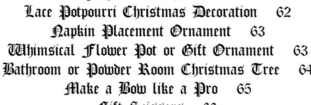

'Twas the Week Before Christmas

'Twas the week before Christmas, when all through the mess
I saw chaos and clutter and felt megastress.
Only seven days left for shopping and such
No time to prepare— there was just too much!

When what to my wondering eyes did appear?
But a hoard of ideas from friends far and near…
Recipes scrumptious, quick, tried and true,
Decoration ideas that were easy to do!
And crafts clean and simple for both old and young
I knew in a moment my planning was done.

When Christmas day came and the family arrived,
Amidst festive decor, Christmas cheer thrived.
The culinary crafts warmed the hearts of my kin
And blessed all the family without and within.

So I share with you these secrets confessed
In hopes that your Christmas will be without stress!

8

Introduction

Simplicity is the hallmark and the theme of this book. Christmastime should not be a time of stress and anxiety; yet many of us find ourselves in frenetic chaos just days before Christmas. In our desperate attempts to put the finishing touches on our Christmas shopping, we press to the limits of our coping skills and wind up exhausted or sick moments before or immediately following the big event. We've all been there. Yet every year we resolve to plan months in advance and take on only those Christmas tasks that can be easily and inexpensively handled. Somehow, things always seem to go awry and again we find ourselves right back on the Christmas stress treadmill, undertaking elaborate, time consuming and costly creations.

We all want our homes decorated to look like a page from *Better Homes and Gardens* that would be the envy of even Martha Stewart. We strive to perfect every detail of every recipe for our Christmas parties, open houses and family meals, but time and cost take their toll on the average household; hence, the creation of this book.

You can have that beautifully decorated home, scrumptious meal and keep the children happy too without having a nervous breakdown! The crafts in this book are all easy; require about a half hour's time each to make, and cost under $10.00. (A few basic tools like a glue gun are well worth purchasing and should last a lifetime.) The recipes are tried and true from old traditional, treasured family recipes.

If you can, plan well in advance to give yourself time to enjoy family, friends and festivities. Don't panic if crafts and decorations don't come out exactly like those in this book. Use your individuality and creativity; but above all, relax and enjoy yourself. Remember, this is your holiday, too.!

"This your idea of a good old-fashioned
Christmas — turkey pizza?"

Recipes

Definitely for cheese lovers!

BRENDA'S CHEESY CRAB APPETIZERS

1 pkg. of 8 English Muffins (split in two)
1 crushed clove of garlic
2-7 oz. cans (200 g ea.) crabmeat

1 cup (250 mL) Cheese Whiz
1/3 cup (75 mL) softened butter
1 1/2 tsp. (7 mL) salad dressing

Mix the crabmeat with the crushed garlic, Cheese Whiz, softened butter and salad dressing until smooth and creamy. Spread the mixture on the English Muffins, and slice into thirds. Bake in a 400°F (200°C) oven for 10 minutes or until golden brown. This recipe can be prepared 1 day ahead, covered and kept in the refrigerator until baking time. Makes 48 appetizers.

RUSS'S CHEDDAR CHEESE DIP

Helpful Hint
Brush a little oil on the grater before grating and cheese will wash off the grater easily

4.8 oz. (120 g) pkg. cream cheese
1/4 cup (50 mL) diced raw onion
1 lb. (500 g) shredded cheddar cheese
3/4 cup (175 mL) whipping cream

cayenne pepper to taste
salt and pepper to taste
Worcestershire Sauce to taste
2 tbsp. (25 mL) dry sherry (optional)

Mix all the ingredients together until it is a mousse consistency. A food processor or blender is useful for mixing. Use with your favorite crackers and vegetables. Makes enough dip for approximately 20 people. Make ahead, but bring from fridge 30 min. before using to soften.

Brenda's Cheesy Crab Appetizers

Russ's Cheddar Cheese Dip

This recipe is simple, moist and delicious.

TERESA'S TURKEY STUFFING

1/4 cup (60 mL) butter
1 large, chopped onion
2 large stems of chopped celery (with leaves)
3 tbsp. (50 mL) chopped parsley
1 cup (250 mL) chopped mushrooms

salt & pepper to taste
1 egg, slightly beaten
1/3 cup (80 mL) milk
half a loaf (or more) of day-old bread cut into cubes

Melt butter slowly in a large frying pan. Add onion and cook only till it is soft and slightly transparent. Add celery, and mix with onion. Next, stir in the chopped mushrooms. Turn off the heat, but keep the pan on the warm burner. Add the bread cubes; sprinkle the parsley and salt and pepper over the bread. Mix thoroughly with the vegetables. Take the pan off the stove. Beat the egg and milk together and pour it over the bread. The mixture should be moist, but not soggy. If you prefer a crunchy stuffing, add 1/3 cup (80 mL) chopped walnuts or pine nuts to the bread mixture. This stuffing can be made a day in advance and kept in a covered bowl in the fridge.

> *Helpful Hint: Cranberries*
> *If you have purchased more cranberries than you need, freeze them! They can be taken from the freezer when needed and used in your favorite recipes. No defrosting necessary.*

BETTER THAN BAKED POTATOES

4 large baking potatoes
1/4 cup (50 mL) olive oil or melted butter

1/4 cup (50 mL) parmesan cheese
1 tbsp. (5 mL) paprika

Halve the potatoes lengthwise. In a dish, mix parmesan cheese with paprika. Spread oil or butter on cut side of potato. Dip each potato in cheese mixture and bake on greased pan, at 375°F (190°C), cut side down, for 45-60 min.

Teresa's Turkey Stuffing

Better Than Baked Potatoes

15

This recipe will make anyone a brussels sprout lover!

BRUSSELS SPROUTS AU GRATIN

2 lb. (1 kg) brussels sprouts	1 tsp. (5 mL) Dijon mustard
3 tbsp. (50 mL) butter	3/4 tsp. (4 mL) salt
3 tbsp. (50 mL) flour	1/4 tsp. (2 mL) pepper
2 cups (500 mL) milk	1 cup (250 mL) shredded sharp cheddar cheese

Clean brussels sprouts and cook in large pan of boiling water until just crisp (7-9 min.) Drain and rinse in cold water. Blot moisture with a towel; cool, and cut into halves.

In a pan, melt butter over medium heat. Stir in flour and cook, stirring for 1 min. Add milk and cook, stirring for 3-5 min. until smooth and thickened. Blend in the mustard, salt and pepper. Remove from heat and stir in half of the cheese and blend until melted. Carefully stir in brussels sprouts.

In a greased 11" x 7" (2 L) baking dish, spoon in the brussels sprouts. (This recipe can be prepared to this point and covered and refrigerated for 1 day.) When ready to use, top the sprouts with the remaining cheddar cheese. Bake in a preheated, 375˚F (190˚C) oven for 30 minutes. Makes 8 servings.

Helpful Hint
If cheese dries out, grate it and use it as a recipe ingredient.

Brussels Sprouts au Gratin

This is an old family favorite that I make every Thanksgiving and Christmas.

BUTTERNUT SQUASH GRAND MARNIER

2 small butternut squash, cut up
2 tbsp. (25 mL) butter
1/4 cup (50 mL) sweetened condensed milk

1/2 tsp. (2 mL) salt
1/4 cup (50 mL) frozen orange juice concentrate
3 tbsp. (50 mL) Grand Marnier

In a large saucepan filled with water, boil the squash until softened, mash and mix with salt, butter and undiluted orange juice. Spoon into a casserole. This recipe can be prepared to this point one day ahead. When ready to use, cover with condensed milk mixed with Grand Marnier. Bake in a 350°F (180°C) oven for 15 min. and then serve. (Bake a little longer — until thoroughly heated — if you have just removed it from the refrigerator.)

Helpful Hint
You can make this one day ahead of time. Just wrap it and keep it in the refrigerator!

Butternut Squash Grand Marnier

JUSTINE'S ACADIAN TOURTIÈRE

This old family recipe is quite different from the standard tourtière because the meat is not ground up, but cut into cubes. Note the simplicity of this recipe. The taste is superb because the pie is moist, not dry and crumbly. This has been a hit in our family and a time-honored Christmas Eve tradition.

Pastry recipe for 2 pies
2 lb. (1000 g) pork shoulder, cubed
2 lb. (1000 g) stewing beef, cubed
2-3 large cooking onions, diced

salt & pepper to taste
2 tbsp. (25 mL) flour
2 tbsp. (25 mL) cornstarch
water

Place cubed pork, beef and onions in a large stewing pot or Dutch Oven. Fill the pot with water to cover the meat, and sprinkle with salt and pepper. Bring to a boil, then simmer on low heat for 1-1/2 hours, and continue to fill the pot with water as it evaporates. The meat should be tender and should break with a fork when it is done. Make a smooth paste with flour, cornstarch and water, and thicken the meat liquid with this mixture. Place the meat and thickened liquid in an unbaked pastry shell. Cover with the pastry top and make a few slits to let the steam escape. Bake in a preheated 375°F (190°C) oven for about 30 minutes, or until golden brown. Makes 2 pies.

> *Helpful Hint: Pastry Dough and Pies*
> •*If pastry clings to rolling pin, place the rolling pin in the freezer and chill before flouring.*
>
> •*When baking a pie, put it in an oven browning bag and cut a few slits in the bag and twist shut. Place on a cookie sheet and bake 10 minutes longer than the baking time. Crust will turn golden brown and your oven remains spotless.*

Justine's Acadian Tourtière

DECADENT BUTTER TART SQUARES

1/2 cup (125 mL) soft butter

1/3 cup (75 mL) sugar

1 cup (250 mL) all-purpose flour

2 eggs

1 cup (250 mL) brown sugar

2 tbsp. (25 mL) flour

1/2 tsp. (2 mL) baking powder

1/2 tsp. (2 mL) vanilla

1/2 cup (125 mL) raisins

1/2 cup (125 mL) chopped walnuts

For crust, combine butter, sugar and flour with a fork and press into a 9" (23 cm) square pan. Bake at 350°F (180°C) for 15 min. For topping, combine remaining ingredients. Pour over baked crust and return to oven and bake another 20-25 min. Cool and cut into squares.

Helpful Hint: Cake & Pie Pans
•*Instead of flour, dust baking pans with cocoa so cakes and squares won't have that white floury look.*
•*Take cake out of oven & set it briefly on a damp cloth to make the cake come loose from pan.*

AARON'S NO-BAKE CHOCOLATE PEANUT KRISPIES

1/2 cup (125 mL) packed brown sugar

1/2 cup (125 mL) corn syrup

1/2 cup (125 mL) peanut butter

1 tbsp. (12 mL) butter

2 cups (500 mL) rice crisp cereal

1/2 cup (125 mL) peanuts (salted and halved)

2 tbsp. (25 mL) butter

2 tbsp. (25 mL) unsweetened cocoa

2 tbsp. (25 mL) milk

1/2 tsp. (2 mL) salt

1/2 tsp. (2 mL) vanilla

1 1/2 cup (375 mL) icing sugar

Grease an 8" (20 cm) square pan. Mix brown sugar, corn syrup and peanut butter in a sauce pan over low heat to dissolve. Add butter and blend. Stir in rice crisp cereal and peanuts and pack into the pan. For icing, heat butter, cocoa and milk in a saucepan and dissolve over low heat. Blend in remaining ingredients. Spread icing over the crust. Place in refrigerator and cut into squares when firm. Store unused squares in an air-tight container in refrigerator.

Hilda's Easy Lemon Squares

Call It Your Own Fruitcake

Decadent Butter Tart Squares

Overnight Meringues

Aaron's Chocolate Peanut Krispies

Shannon's Peanut S'Mores

Brendan's Favorite Shortbread Cookies

23

Sometimes the easiest recipe produces the best results!

OVERNIGHT MERINGUES

2 egg whites
3/4 cup (175 mL) super fine sugar

1/2 tsp. (2 mL) vanilla
1/4 tsp. (1 mL) cream of tartar

Preheat oven to 350°F (180°C). Beat egg whites until foamy. Beat in cream of tartar and gradually add the sugar. Beat at high speed for 5 min. until stiff shiny peaks form. Fold in vanilla and drop from teaspoon onto a foil-lined cookie sheet. Place in oven and turn off the heat. Leave overnight or at least 8 hours. *VARIATIONS*: Add 1/2 cup (125 mL) of walnuts or pecans or chocolate chips to the meringues. A few drops of food coloring can also be added for a festive look. Makes about 3 dozen cookies.

BRENDAN'S ALL-TIME FAVORITE SHORTBREAD COOKIES

1/2 cup (125 mL) corn starch
1/2 cup (125 mL) icing sugar

1 cup (250 mL) all purpose flour
3/4 cup (175 mL) unsalted soft butter

Preheat oven to 350°F (150°C). Sift together corn starch, icing sugar and flour. Gradually mix in butter until dough is soft. With floured palms of your hands, shape into 1" (2.5 cm) balls. Place on UNGREASED cookie sheet about 1 1/2" (4 cm) apart. Flatten dough with floured fork. Bake for 15-20 min or until edges are lightly browned. Makes about 2 dozen cookies. (Add quartered red and green maraschino cherries to the cookies before baking, to add a seasonal, festive look.)

Helpful Hint: Gift Containers
Buy cake boxes, doilies and cardboard cake bases at cake decorating or craft stores. Your own baked goods are well received when they are presented in attractively packaged and wrapped boxes.

HILDA'S EASY LEMON SQUARES WITH BASIC BUTTER ICING

3 lemons
1 can sweetened condensed milk
1 box Graham Cracker Squares

Squeeze the juice from lemons and mix with sweetened condensed milk. Line an 8" (20 cm) square pan with Graham Cracker squares, breaking the crackers where necessary to adequately fit the pan. Spread 1/2 the lemon mixture on top. Cover the lemon mixture with

Helpful Hint: Lemons
Submerging a lemon in hot water for 15 min. before squeezing will yield almost twice the amount of juice.
If you need only a few drops of juice, prick one end with a fork and squeeze the desired amount. Return the lemon to the refrigerator and it will be as good as new.

another layer of crackers. Repeat this method again, ending with the crackers. Place in the refrigerator to set and crackers become soft. Spread icing over set lemon squares and cut into small 1" (2.5 cm) squares. If icing is not desired, end with the lemon mixture and sprinkle instead with a dusting of Graham Cracker Crumbs. Then cut into squares.

BASIC BUTTER ICING

3 tbsp. (50 mL) soft butter
1-2 tbsp. (15-25 mL) milk

1 1/2 cups (375 mL) icing sugar
1 tsp. (5 mL) vanilla

Cream butter and gradually beat in 1/2 the sugar. Add milk and remaining sugar and blend until smooth. Blend in vanilla.

SHANNON'S NO-BAKE PEANUT S'MORES

1 pkg. (300 g) semi-sweet chocolate chips

1 can sweetened condensed milk

2 cups (500 mL) rice crisp cereal

1 cup (250 mL) peanuts

In a saucepan over low heat, melt chocolate chips with condensed milk. Remove from heat and stir in rice crisps and peanuts. Drop by teaspoon onto wax paper-lined baking sheet. Chill until firm—about 2 hours. Makes about 4 dozen.

EASY WINTER COMPOTE

2 cups (500 mL) frozen rhubarb

12 oz. pkg. (300 g) frozen unsweetened raspberries or strawberries

2 pears, cubed

1/2 cup (125 mL) sugar

1/4-1/2 tsp. (1-2 mL) cinnamon

1/4 -1/3 cup (50-75 mL) rum or brandy (optional)

Helpful Hint
Reserve some of your compote for use as a hostess gift by spooning into a preserving jar and decorating the lid with Christmas fabric, colorful ribbons, and jingle bells.

Rinse rhubarb under cold water until ice crystals melt. Place in a large, microwaveable bowl. Add berries and pears. In a separate bowl, blend sugar and cinnamon. Sprinkle over fruit. Cover and microwave on high for 15-18 min., stirring every 5 minutes. Stir in the rum or brandy and spoon over your favorite ice cream. Makes about 4 cups.

WENDY'S OLD ENGLISH RASPBERRY TRIFLE

Two 15 oz. cans (425 g ea.) frozen, whole raspberries
Two 15 oz. cans (425 g ea.) prepared custard
One 3 oz. box (85 g) raspberry jelly powder
1/4 cup (60 mL) sweet sherry (optional)

1 large prepared jelly roll
2 cups (500 mL) whipping cream
1 tsp. (5 mL) vanilla
3 tsp. (15 mL) sugar

Thaw frozen raspberries reserving juice. Cut jelly roll into slices, and line the bottom of a large bowl. (Clear glass or crystal bowl is especially attractive, as it shows the layers of color in this trifle.) Prepare the jelly powder with 1 cup (250 mL) of boiling water, plus 1 cup (250 mL)

Helpful Hint: Chocolate Curls
Large chocolate curls can be made by using a plain milk chocolate bar that has been left at room temperature, and peeled using a potato peeler.

of the reserved raspberry juice, and pour this liquid over the jelly roll, making sure it is thoroughly soaked. If using, pour 1/4 cup (50 mL) of sherry over top. Refrigerate for 2 hours. Pour the raspberries on next, followed by the cans of custard. Refrigerate again until set. Prepare the whipping cream and mix with the vanilla and sugar and place on top of the trifle. Garnish with shredded or curled chocolate.

Wendy's Old English Raspberry Trifle

CALL IT YOUR OWN FRUITCAKE

No time to make those delicious, complicated, time-consuming fruitcakes? Here's an easy way to have your cake and eat it too! Buy a good quality, uniced fruitcake about one month before you need it. To ripen, poke holes with a skewer into the cake and add a small amount of brandy or rum. Wrap the spiked cake in a cheesecloth, then wrap waxed paper around the cake, followed by a layer of tin foil. Place the wrapped cake in an airtight container and store in the refrigerator or a cool, dry place. Every week before Christmas, unwrap the cake and pour more alcohol onto the cake and wrap and store again. A few days before serving, buy some almond paste and evenly spread over the cake. Wrap again and store. Just before serving, prepare butter icing (see Lemon Squares recipe, p. 25) and spread this icing over the almond paste. Decorate with red and green maraschino cherries. Nobody will know you didn't slave over a hot stove to produce this masterpiece. This cake will store beautifully in the freezer, ready for unexpected guests.

Helpful Hints: Fruitcake

Refrigerate the cake a few hours before serving to make slicing easier. Use a very sharpe knife and wipe blade clean with hot water between slices.

Fruitcake Refresher: To revive a slightly stale fruitcake, simply flip the cake upside down, skewer a few holes in it and pour some frozen orange juice into the holes. When the juice melts, it will moisten the cake by blending throughout without messy drips. When the juice has melted, flip the cake rightside up, slice and serve!

Helpful Hint: Bananas
This is a great recipe to use for over-ripened bananas!

ELEANOR'S BEST BANANA BREAD

1 cup (250 mL) sugar
3 ripened, mashed bananas
4 tbsp. (60 mL) melted butter
1 1/2 cups (375 mL) all-purpose flour

1/4 tsp. (1 mL) salt
1 tsp. (5 mL) baking soda
2 eggs, slightly beaten

Preheat oven to 350°F (180°C). Grease and flour an 8" (20 cm) loaf pan. In a small bowl, mix together flour, salt and baking soda; set aside. In another medium bowl, mash bananas; mix with sugar and beaten eggs. Blend dry ingredients with banana mixture and melted butter. Stir until just mixed. Place in loaf pan and tap the pan on the counter a few times to release air bubbles. Bake in oven for 45-50 min. or until golden brown and centre pops up when gently touched.

Variations: Add 1/2 cup (125 mL) of chopped walnuts or raisins or your favorite fruit or nuts.

GARY'S YUMMY BACON AND CHEESE MUFFINS

These muffins are not only great for breakfast and brunches, but for snacks and treats anytime.

1 egg	8 slices of bacon - cooked & chopped
1/2 tsp. (2 mL) salt	1 tbsp.(15 mL) bacon fat reserved from cooked bacon
3 tbsp. (50 mL) butter	1^1/2 cups (375 mL) shredded cheddar cheese
2 tbsp. (30 mL) sugar	2 cups (500 mL) all purpose flour
1 cup (250 mL) milk	1 tbsp. (15 mL) baking powder

Preheat oven to 400˚F (200˚C). Grease & flour or paper-line 9-12 muffin cups. In a large bowl, blend flour, sugar and baking powder and salt. Stir in cheese and bacon. In a small bowl, combine egg, milk, butter and bacon drippings. Add dry ingredients to liquid ingredients and stir just until moistened. Spoon batter into muffin cups and bake for 25-30 min.

Helpful Hint: Revived Muffins
Dip stale muffins quickly in cold milk & heat in a moderate oven

Gary's Bacon & Cheese Muffins

Eleanor's Best Banana Bread

33

Decorations

printed with permission from Andrea L. Mori-Mickus

DECORATING YOUR DINING ROOM

If you have the space, don't leave out your dining room as a room for special decorations. It adds to the overall look of Christmas in your home.

Our buffet was decorated with 1 string of 35 mini lights, pine boughs and flowered garland.

WHITE CHRISTMAS TREE

Surprisingly, there are only five types of decorations on this six foot tree, topped off by one large, gold wire-rimmed ribbon.

MATERIALS:

1 large bunch of snowflake gypsophilia, divided into small bunches and wired at the ends. Insert directly into tree branches
60 cream colored woodflowers -preferably with wire ends to fasten on to tree branch
pink or white tulle and metallic paper for the tree skirt. (Place the tulle around the bottom of the tree first, then wrap the tulle loosely with the metallic paper.)

2 sets of 100 mini lights
5 pkgs. of gold star glitter garland
1 spool of white tulle

Helpful Hint:
Decorating the Christmas Tree

Use green pipe cleaners to fasten tree lights onto branches.

If you are using "icicles" for decorations, place the box in the freezer a few days before using to avoid static cling.

DECK THE HALLS

This hall and bannister are enhanced with a grapevine wreath decorated with large dried flowers and bunches of deep green myrtle. The bannister has a swag of imitation pine roping (much neater than fresh cedar roping). Pink tulle, gold glitter garland and blue ornaments adorn the pale blue entryway. Some inexpensive, battery operated mini lights are inserted into the greenery on both the pine roping and wreath adding a soft glow in the evening.

This hurricane centerpiece is easier to make than it looks. The base is a buckbrush wreath and decorations of gold wash eucalyptus, sprayed and glittered pink lilies and assorted silk flowers are simply inserted into the wreath. Nothing is wired or glued to allow for changes year by year if desired.

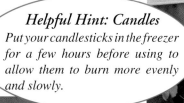

Helpful Hint: Candles
Put your candlesticks in the freezer for a few hours before using to allow them to burn more evenly and slowly.

To complete the decoration of a poinsettia, simply wrap the pot with metallic paper or colourful fabric to complement your room. Bring the wrapping up kerchief-style and secure with a colorful cord. This also eliminates mess when watering the plant.

FIRESIDE MOTIF

A grapevine wreath with white and red tiny flowers, pinecones and gold glitter garland over the mantelpiece laden with assorted white, green and red candles, surrounded by green pine branches, red berries and gold garland depicts a warm atmosphere in this oak-panelled room.

Our hearth, decorated with a small green pole tied with large flower preserved gypsophilia, adorned with a colorful Christmas ornament is a quick and easy enhancement to this fireplace hearth.

To complete this warm fireplace effect, a red basket of sprayed and glittered pine cones, shiny apples and tartan ribbons are added. Even our little "Scotty" dog dons a tartan ribbon to add to the design.

Helpful Hint: Wreaths

Any plain grapevine wreath can be easily decorated with silk or dried flowers, holly, berries, pinecones, eucalyptus, colorful ribbons, tiny white lovebirds, bells or whatever your imagination can create.

41

The Corner Country Cupboard

Our warm country kitchen is enhanced by splashes of bright red color. The corner country cupboard is decorated with bunches of boxwood branches and red berries. Mini lights placed among the boughs add evening charm to this cozy room. Fruit, berries, tulle and curled ribbon decorate our kitchen Xmas tree.

This glorious coffee grinder, made in Poughkeepsie N. Y. and found in an antique shop in cottage country of Northern Ontario, is gaily decorated with a 12" (30 cm) thistle tree, spray painted white and decorated with miniature red apples and red raffia ribbon.

Decorate a country coffee table by simply arranging candles of various sizes on old-fashioned candle holders. Add wired holly berries to the candle holders for a festive look.

Helpful Hint: Candles
If your candles are too thin for the holder, wrap a rubber band around the base before placing in the holder; or use a little florist's clay in the bottom of the holder to secure the candle in place.

GILDED CHRISTMAS TREE

This tree is so effective, yet so simple and elegant. All the decorations are inserted into the branches for easy removal and redecorating.

MATERIALS
small twig tree
gold short curly tamboo
gold artichokes
gold wash eucalyptus
bleached woodflowers
gold Nigella Orientalis
gold Holly Oak
gold wire garland

All these materials are available at specialty craft stores.

Helpful Hint:
Christmas Light Storage:
Save the cardboard tubes of wrapping paper to store extension cords inside, or store tree lights around the tube to prevent them from getting tangled. Push the plug into the tube, then wrap the lights around the outside and secure the end with a rubber band.

ELEGANT BRANCH SWAG
This fruited swag decorated a plain
kitchen door that lead to a basement.

MATERIALS
white and gold-edged wire ribbon
red berries
assorted silk flowers
gold wash eucalyptus
tiny gold ribbons to fasten the wire
ribbon in place
tiny bundles of gypsophilia
tiny bundles of German Status

WHITE SWAG
with
GOLD & TULLE BOW

MATERIALS

l bunch of white glittered Jay Branches (available at craft supplies stores)
wire-rimmed, gold weaving ribbon
white tulle

Divide the Jay Branches and gather them in the center with florist wire or pipe cleaner. Insert lengths of white tulle throughout the branches. Accent with a double layer of white tulle and gold ribbon. If you're all thumbs when it comes to bow creations, many craft supplies stores will be happy to create it for you.

COUNTRY BRANCH SWAG

This back door of a country home was enhanced by a simple twig swag that was very effective.

MATERIALS

1 small twig door tree
1 pkg. of natural raffia, cut and tied into tiny bows and tucked gently onto the branches
1 large colorful velvet bow

Helpful Hint: Raffia Ribbons
It might be helpful to spread newspaper on your work area before cutting the raffia to avoid messy bits on your floor or table.

THE OUTDOOR SCENE

Pine roping, red velvet ribbons, mini lights and candlesticks enhance the outdoors of this home. The front door is decorated with a simple pine wreath with bright red cherries wired on. A cheerful French horn and red velvet ribbons accent this easy-to-make wreath.

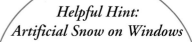

Helpful Hint:
Artificial Snow on Windows

Before spraying artificial snow on windows, first spray the window with cooking oil spray. The "snow" will easily wipe off when the holiday is over.

The rural mailbox is decorated with a freshly-cut bunch of yew, tied and accented with a large red velvet ribbon to complete the look of the front area.

For the porch, a three foot (0.91 m) artificial tree decorated with gold glitter garland and mini lights add a welcome look of color and light to the doorstep.

The snow-covered back garden post, usually holding a colorful pot of impatiens in the summertime, now holds a straw wreath with honey-glued bird seed accented with a tartan ribbon. It makes an attractive, yet functional bird feeder.

CANDLES IN A BAG - MEXICAN FAROLITOS

I first saw this interesting lantern-light effect while on a family Christmas vacation in Florida. Anticipating sunny beaches and tropical flowers, I wondered whether Floridians acknowledged Christmas with any of the enthusiasm or pageantry which we enjoy in the northern climates. To my delight I discovered that they really do know how to prepare and decorate for Christmas — perhaps the absence of snow and traditional Christmas settings prompts them to invent new and creative ways to induce the Christmas spirit!

On Christmas Eve, the residents of the community where we were vacationing lined both sides of the streets with plastic bags. Each bag was filled with sand and a tiny candle inserted inside. At dusk, the candles were lit and the effect was breathtaking! All the streets were illuminated with the soft glow of candlelight flickering and casting shimmering shadows through the white plastic bags.

By the end of the evening, the candles had burned themselves out and the residual candlewax was safely melted into the sand. By morning, the bags had been removed and all that remained was the memory of a magical Christmas Eve.

Apparently, this custom originated in Mexico where *farolitos* or little lanterns line sidewalks and city squares. You can create this same effect on your own doorstep or laneway to greet your guests and holiday visitors.

MATERIALS:

white plastic or paper bags - enough to space every 2-3 feet (60-90 cm) apart.

sand
tea candles - same number as bags used

Place about 2 cups (500 mL) of sand in the bottom of the bag and place a tea candle in the center.

Helpful Hint: Farolitos
To avoid burning your fingers, use long, wooden matches to light the tiny candles. If sand is hard to find at this time of year, use a bag of kitty litter.

Crafts & Gift Ideas

Crafts & Gift Ideas

MINI TABLE-TOP CHRISTMAS TREE

This tiny 12 inch (30 cm) Christmas tree is perfect for a desk, side table or small chest of drawers. Lightly snow spray a plain, artificial tree, assembled on a stand (found at all craft stores), and wire, glue, or intersperse tiny bunches of baby's breath, silk flowers and gaily-wrapped miniature presents. For the base, wrap a color-coordinated piece of foil and fasten with a bow. Top the tree off with a corresponding bow.

CHRISTMAS TREE ORNAMENTS

Simply fill a glass ball tree ornament with your favorite potpourri. Replace the hook and string a curled ribbon from the hook.

STARCHED LACE & RIBBON ORNAMENT

Buy a 6 inch (15 cm) piece of lace and stiffen it following fabric stiffener directions (stiffener can be bought at any craft supplies store), or buy a prepared starched piece of lace. Pleat the lace accordian-style and fasten in the centre with a piece of wire. Using a glue gun, fasten the lace ends together. Loop a 4 inch (10 cm) piece of ribbon and glue the ends to the back of the lace. Fold and glue another 4 inch (10 cm) piece of ribbon in the center of the lace and glue on a tiny rose ribbon.

54

BIRD'S NEST TREE ORNAMENT

MATERIALS:

3" (7.5 cm) plain, oval, wooden box, available at all craft supplies stores
6" (15 cm) colored roping for hanging the ornament on the tree
brocade, needlepoint, or any fabric suitable to cover the length and width of the box
2 tiny love birds
pine boughs
3 tiny pine cones, berries or beads; faux pearls, ribbons and moss

Using your glue gun, glue the fabric onto the box. Glue the colored roping to each side of the box. Fill the box with the moss. Glue the pine, beads, pine cones, love birds and ribbons in place.

Helpful Hint: Easy Christmas Tree Decorations
For a simple and fast way to decorate your tree, or to fill in the "empty spaces", buy tulle circles of white or complimentary colors of your tree or home. (These tulle circles are usually used in weddings to wrap candied almond favors, available at wedding and craft supplies stores.) Bunch up the tulle slightly by gathering the tulle in the center and insert directly into the branches. This simple and inexpensive idea completes and adds a "lacy" look to your tree. (See the kitchen tree, p42 for an example.

DECORATED PINE CONES

Use complimentary colors of your home to decorate these unique pine cone ornaments.

MATERIALS:

glitter-sprayed pine cones (available at craft supplies stores)
tiny dried or silk flowers
2" wide (5 cm) wire-rimmed ribbon - about 8" (20 cm) for each pine cone
14" (35 cm) length of metallic gold or silver wire for each pine cone
craft pearls

INSTRUCTIONS:

Using the 14" (35 cm) length of gold/silver wire, create a hanger for the ornament by making a 4" (10 cm) loop. Twist the wire around the pine cone several times to secure the hanger.

Make a bow from your wire-edged ribbon and hot glue it to the top of your ornament, cascading the ends of the ribbon down one side of the ornament. Hot glue it in place. Complete the ornament by hot-gluing the silk or dried flowers and craft pearls onto the ornament.

Helpful Hint: Firestarters

Coat your pinecones with paraffin wax to make fast and easy firestarters. Add scented oil to the melted wax to give fragrance to the fire.

BASKETS! BASKETS! AND MORE BASKETS!

Take any size wicker basket and hot glue a length of white eyelet lace to the sides. Hot glue pieces of Spanish moss on top of the lace, followed by berries, flowers and leaves. Hot glue flowers or berries along the handle, then fill the basket with apples, pine cones or gifts of preserves - the list is endless and makes a perfect gift for friends or hostesses.

Helpful Hint: Gift Ideas

For avid readers on your Christmas list, fill a red wicker basket with magazines of special interest to the recipient. A paid subscription to a favorite magazine further enhances the enduring quality of the gift.

57

WALL-MOUNTED BASKET

With the leftover berries from the wicker basket, we decorated a flat, moss-covered, wall-mounted basket. We purchased two tiny white love birds and 20" (50 cm) of 1 1/2 " (3.75 cm) wire-sided white satin ribbon. This ribbon works very easily and keeps its shape as you mold and place the ribbon along the face of the basket. Hot glue in place. Hot glue the red and white berries along one side of the basket. Hot glue the love birds, facing each other, in place. This makes another charming gift.

CINNAMON KITCHEN BASKET

This is a simple way to dress up your kitchen for Christmas. Place silver or gold-sprayed pine cones in a colorful red or green wicker basket. Tie bunches of cinnamon sticks together with bright red ribbons and place them around the pine cones. Take a length of tartan ribbon and wrap the entire basket and tie a bow on top. Add silver or gold tassels to the handles for a finished look.

LINED GIFT BASKETS

Line a small, painted basket with Christmas-colored fabric and fill it with assorted treats to make a perfect gift. This white basket was lined with simple red tissue paper, but fabric cut to fit the size of the basket is also attractive. Fasten a bright bow in place and your gift basket is complete.

Helpful Hints: A Gift Idea
For a friend who loves to sew, fill a basket or tote bag with needles, thread, scissors, patterns, instruction books, taylor's chalk, pins, etc.

59

SPICED TRIVET

The fragrant aroma of spices and potpourri escape when a warm pot of tea or casserole dish is placed on this scented cushion.

MATERIALS:
1/4 yard (22 cm) Christmas printed cotton
1 cup (250 mL) potpourri or spices such as whole cloves
1 yard (1 m) white eyelet lace or cord ribbons (optional)

Cut two 7 1/2" (19 cm) squares of your Christmas fabric. Sew or hot glue the squares and lace together, leaving one side open. Pour spices or potpourri into the opening and stitch or hot glue the remaining opened side. Glue attractive ribbons, flowers or pearls along the top edge for decoration. These scented cushions can also be placed in your linen drawers to give your table linens a beautifully scented fragrance.

> *Helpful Hint: Christmas Scents:*
> *Shortly before guests arrive, simmer spices such as cinnamon and cloves in water for a Christmasy, fragrant aroma.*

POTPOURRI!

POTPOURRI JAR

For a great gift or a scented decoration for your own room, fill a potpourri jar with your favorite scented, colored potpourri. Place a 7" (18 cm) piece of Victorian lace on top and fasten with a pretty satin bow.

SCENTED PLAQUES

Colorful potpourri are placed into laced needlework frames (available at craft and sewing stores). Color-coordinated lace is hot-glued to the back of the frame, and a tiny satin ribbon and rose are hot-glued just beneath the hook. These make great gifts and beautiful for the powder room or bedroom.

POTPOURRI SACHETS

These elegant Victorian lace sachets make a charming hostess gift or decoration for a makeup table, or fragrant packets for your dresser drawers. Simply buy an 8" x 12" (20cm x 30 cm) piece of Victorian lace handkerchief and fill with potpourri. Tie with a satin ribbon and accent with dried flowers.

LACE POTPOURRI CHRISTMAS TREE DECORATION

Buy tiny plastic Christmas balls (available at craft stores). Separate the ball along the seam and fill with potpourri. Place the ball together and cover with a circle of tulle. Bring the tulle upwards and tie with a satin ribbon. The colorful potpourri shows through the plastic and tulle.

NAPKIN PLACEMENT ORNAMENT

To adorn your Christmas dining room table, add these beautiful ornaments to each napkin or plate. Purchase a Christmas decoration that would enhance the color of your table setting. Wire or glue a satin bow to the ornament and your table is complete.

WHIMSICAL FLOWER POT OR GIFT ORNAMENT

To add charm to your poinsettia or gift bag, include a charming Christmas ornament. Our little mouse ornament is attached to a two foot (60 cm) stick with florist tape. A beautiful Victorian lace bow is tied directly underneath to hide the tape and to add a touch of elegance.

BATHROOM OR POWDER ROOM
CHRISTMAS TREE

Don't forget your bathroom when you're decorating your home for Christmas. This delightful soap-tree brightens up a guest powder room with cheerful color and scent. It takes no time to make and is perfect for a hostess or Christmas gift.

MATERIALS:

12" (30 cm) styrofoam cone
4 yards (4 m) of green moire silk ribbon, 1 3/8 " (3.5 cm) wide
40 colourful, tiny, decorator soaps
forty 2" corsage pearl pins
Dressmaker straight pins, 1 3/16" (3 cm)

Cut silk into 3" (7.5 cm) lengths; fold in half and pin using dressmaker pins to the cone. This gives the cone a "pine tree" look. Using the pearl pins, insert the pin through the soap and attach to bare spots on the tree giving it a "decorated" look. Your tree is finished and ready to adorn your bathroom.

Helpful Hint: Soaps

When the decorator soaps become old and dusty, fill a pint jar with one-half cup (125 mL) of water and place the soaps a few at a time in the water. Leave for a few days to soften. When the soaps have softened, place the contents of the jar in your food processor and whirl for 30 seconds. Pour the liquid soap into a pump-style dispenser, and voila! instant liquid soap. To clean the food processor, rinse in hot water to get the soap out. This method is great for tiny scraps of hand soap, too.

MAKE A BOW LIKE A PRO!

We've all seen those beautiful, professionally made Christmas bows and wished we could make them too. Now you can with this little trick.

MATERIALS:
3 pieces of velvet ribbon - 20" long and 3" wide (50 cm x 7.5 cm)
1 piece of velvet ribbon - 8" long and 3" wide (20 cm x 7.5 cm)
1 same colored pipe cleaner
stapler

Make a bow by gathering two ends of the ribbon together. Repeat this process using the second piece of 20" long ribbon. "Scrunch" the ribbon in the middle and staple in place. For the centre, loop the 8" ribbon and staple in the centre. For the streamer, take the remaining 20" long ribbon and scrunch and staple in the center. Gather all 4 pieces together and fasten with the pipe cleaner, inserting the pipe cleaner through the center ribbon to hide the pipe cleaner.

Helpful Hint: Ribbons
To revive a wrinkled piece of ribbon, simply run the ribbon through a heated curling iron and your ribbon is instantly smooth again. For velvet ribbons, run them across a hot light bulb to smooth out the wrinkles, without crushing the fabric.

GIFT SCISSORS

For friends on your Christmas list who are crafts enthusiasts or who knit or sew, this useful and lovely tool will be warmly received. Simply buy a decorator pair of dressmaker scissors, or any other tool that would be appropriate, and tie a lace ribbon to it. Hot glue flowered appliques to the ribbon and the tool to make an attractive gift.

Helpful Hint: Containers
For a gift, or for travel purposes, save those 35mm film cannisters and turn them into containers for needles, tiny buttons, lace appliques, etc.

LINDA'S "QUILTED" CHRISTMAS CARDS

This craft is a little more time-consuming, but for those who love to sew, it is worth the extra effort. This is also a great project to do with your children, to introduce them to sewing, while creating a delightful craft.

TOOLS:
sewing machine
scissors
cutting mat
x-acto knife
needles and assorted
colored thread
pencil and eraser
glue stick

MATERIALS FOR EACH CARD:

Scraps of Christmas print fabric
2 sheets of notepaper and envelope
for each card (we used 6" x 8" or 15 x 20 cm paper)
sequins, beads, ribbons, etc., for decoration
paper towels

HOW TO MAKE QUILTED CARDS:

Two sheets of any medium-weight paper are used for each "quilted" card. The cards are a sandwich of 4 layers: three for the card front and one for the back. When the card is finished, the fabric and paper towel padding are between layers 2 and 3, and layer 3 is glued to layer 2 to hide the paper towel and the back of the stitching.

Step-by-Step

1. **Fold two sheets of note paper in half.**
   This creates 4 LAYERS for the card and looks like a little book.
2. **Draw or trace the shape(s) onto LAYER 1 lightly in pencil.**
3. **Cut out the shape(s) through LAYERS 1 and 2 only** using an X-acto knife and cutting mat.

   Gently erase any remnants of the pencil line
4. **Cut piece(s) of fabric**
   to place under the opening, using the paper cut-out as a pattern. The fabric should be at least 1/4" (6.25 mm) bigger than the opening all the way around.
5. **Cut 3 or more layers of paper towel** approximately 3" x 5" (75 mm x 125 mm) to pad the fabric piece(s)
6. **Position the fabric(s) and the paper towel** under the opening(s) in layers 1 and 2.

7. Stitch around the shape(s) with the sewing machine. Sew through LAYERS 1 and 2 AND the fabric AND the paper towel, being sure to keep everything aligned with the opening(s).
Use straight or zigzag or decorative stitches. Use needle down to pivot at corners. Cut the threads leaving long ends to pull through to the back. Tie thread ends on the back to secure; snip off excess. Trim fabric to neaten the back if necessary.

8. Add handsewn details like sequins and bows. Leave the knots on the back of LAYER 2 and plan your route to eliminate long jumps of thread.

9. Complete your design on LAYER 1 with stickers and drawn/painted details, if required.

10. Glue LAYER 3 to LAYER 2 with the glue stick to hide the threads and paper towel.

11. Write your greeting on LAYER 1 and/or LAYER 4 using your colored pens. If you need inspiration, look at commercial greeting cards for verse and phrases you can use or adapt. Christmas carols and poems are good too: *Jingle Bells*, *'Twas the Night Before Christmas* and more.

12. Put your maker's mark on the back of LAYER 4. Don't forget to take credit for your creation!

By Linda 1994

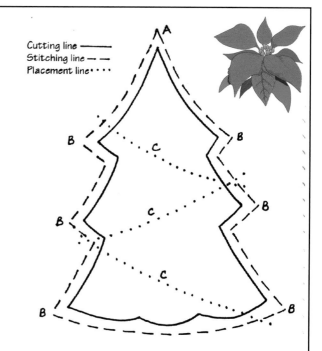

Cutting line ——
Stitching line — —
Placement line • • • •

One cut-out and one piece of fabric make a tree that is fun to decorate with a sequin or sticker for the star at A, and hand sewn sequins for ornaments at B. Ribbon, lace or rickrack can be placed on lines similar to C to look like garland.

Place 'garlands' on the fabric before machine stitching to eliminate the need to sew by hand.
Try drawing other shapes too. A simple triangle can look very tree-like.

Kids' Crafts

Kids' Crafts

Shannon's snowman the day after…

EASY GINGERBREAD HOUSES KIDS CAN MAKE THEMSELVES!

Have you ever been to a bakery or craft store where elaborate gingerbread houses were elegantly displayed in store windows? Have your kids ever whined that they wanted you to make an exact replica of this impossible mansion, or buy one at exorbitant prices? Have you ever been so guilt-ridden by your family to actually attempt to create this non-creatable nightmare? Well, we have the answer to rid you of your unnecessary guilt and still create (or better still, have your kids create) easy, mini-"gingerbread" houses. Actually, these houses are not made from gingerbread at all, but from store-bought, ready-made Graham Crackers - so there's absolutely no baking at all.

INGREDIENTS FOR ONE GINGERBREAD MINI HOUSE

6 Graham Crackers
royal icing (method to follow)
1 box of gumdrops, Smarties and/or jelly beans

72

METHOD FOR A GINGERBREAD MINI HOUSE

Glue Graham Crackers on each seam with prepared royal icing, making 4 walls for the base and 2 crackers glued in a pyramid for the roof. Stick on candies for decorations using a small dollop of royal icing. These make great Christmas gifts from your children to their friends or teachers.

ROYAL ICING
(Makes 2 1/2 cups - 625 mL)
4 cups (1000 mL) icing sugar
1/2 tsp. (2 mL) cream of tartar
3 egg whites

Mix icing sugar and cream of tartar together in medium mixing bowl. Using electric mixer, beat in egg whites for 7 to 10 min. or until icing is thick enough to hold its shape. This icing dries rather quickly, so it's important to make the houses before the icing hardens.

Helpful Hint: Royal Icing
Keep bowl of icing covered with a damp cloth at all times to avoid early drying. Icing can be stored in airtight containers. Do not refrigerate.

73

ICE CREAM CONE
CHRISTMAS TREE

While you're making the royal icing for the "gingerbread" houses, save some for this great craft that even the youngest member of your family can create.

MATERIALS

1 box conical ice cream cones
candies, gumdrops or Smarties
(saved from the gingerbread houses!)
Royal Icing (see p. 73 for recipe)
Green food coloring for icing

Decorate the tree with royal icing and add candied ornaments while icing is still moist.

Helpful Hint:
Ice Cream Cone Trees
This activity is also great for children's birthday or Christmas parties.

74

CHRISTMAS CHOCOLATE CANDIES

We purchased the Christmas microwave candy-making kit which comes complete with chocolate, candy mold, lollipop sticks and plastic wrapping bags. These can be found at any craft store or cake supplies store. Follow the recipe on the box.

When the chocolates are firm, unmold them and individually wrap them in the plastic wrapping bags and tie with a colorful bow. This makes a nice Christmas gift for your children's classmates and friends.

Helpful Hint:Chocolate
To thin hardened or thickened chocolate, add 1 tsp. (5 mL) of vegetable oil to make the chocolate liquid again.

BIRD FEEDERS

Have the kids decorate an outside evergreen for the birds. You can make it a festive occasion by inviting friends and family over to decorate your Christmas bird feeder tree.

MATERIALS:
toilet paper rolls
2-cup jar (500 mL) peanut butter
5 lb (2.3 kg) bag of bird seed
string

1. Cut the string into 1 foot long (30 cm) pieces - same number as toilet rolls. Spread seeds onto a large plate or tray. Spread peanut butter on each toilet roll, to completely cover the roll.

2. Roll the toilet roll onto the plate of seeds to cover the entire roll.

3. Fasten string through the seeded toilet roll and tie a knot.

Helpful Hint: Bird Feeders

1. Use of old toilet paper rolls helps the environment by cutting down on waste.

2. Instead of using old toilet rolls, large pine cones can also be used. Simply spread the peanut butter onto the pine cone as you would the toilet roll and roll the pine cone in bird seeds. Tie the string on the top of the pine cone to hang on the tree. This is an inexpensive and environmentally friendly way to feed the birds and decorate your outdoor tree for winter.

decorators: Laura Collins, Shannon Kelly and Melissa Hardsand

The Chickadee

A chickadee came to my feeder today.
I hoped she would eat.
I hoped she would stay.

She hopped branch to branch
In the snowy spruce tree
Pecked lunch from the feeder
And chirped merrily

Then as our cat
Crept close to the tree
The bird flew away
Singing chick-a-dee-dee
— Shannon Kelly

BUSY DAY SNOWMEN CRAFTS FOR KIDS

❶

INVITATION TO A SNOWMAN OR ANYTIME PARTY

Draw a picture of a snowman on folded paper. Cut out the shape of the snowman, color and add the invitation on the inside.

② FLUFFY SNOWMEN

Using makeup remover pads, glue 6 pads together, pyramid style, to make a snowman shape. Decorate and color.

③ SNOWMAN PLACEMATS

Cut out snowman shapes from sheets of large white paper. Decorate and color. To laminate your placemat for re-use, wrap cellophane paper around the placemat and glue or tape at the back.

Helpful Hint: Kids Paint

Using a pump-spray bottle, mix water with a teaspoon (5 mL) of food colouring. Kids can have a ball spray painting snow and decorating snow-laden evergreens.

79